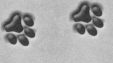

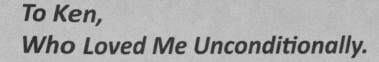

To Ken,
Who Loved Me Unconditionally.

Why Dogs Are...

Written By Tana Thompson
Illustrated By Marita Gentry

Kendall Neff Publishing

Carpenter's Son Publishing

a **FOUR DAYS LATE** project
of Kendall Neff Publishing

www.KendallNeff.com

Author: Tana Thompson

Illustrator: Marita Gentry

Copy Editor: Amy S. Royal

Layout/Design: Jim Ware

Print Agent: Madelyn Spiegelman

Marketing/PR: Cheryl Monkhouse

Website: Chris Horne

Special Efforts: Adrienne A. Isakovic
                 Violet A. Guerrero

Publisher's Cataloging-in-Publication data

Thompson, Tana.

   Why dogs are…/ written by Tana Thompson ;
   illustrated by Marita Gentry.

   p. cm.

   ISBN 978-0-9891624-0-1

   Summary : God uses a dog to teach a very special
   child some very special lessons.

[1. Dogs --Fiction. 2. Guide dogs--Fiction.
3. God --Fiction. 4. Blind children --Fiction.
5. Deaf children --Fiction.] I. Gentry, Marita. Title.

PZ7.T3814 Wh 2013

[E] --dc23   2013905697

ISBN: 978-0-9891624-0-1
Library of Congress Control Number: 2013905697

Kendall Neff Publishing in association with
Carpenter's Son Publishing

256.368.1559

Publr@KendallNeff.com

www.KendallNeff.com

100% of the Net Profits from the sale of this book
are given to charities and organizations that support
animals and their interactions with individuals,
organizations, and situations.
See our website www.WhyDogsAre.com for a list of
recipients.

This book is available to charitable and volunteer
organizations (at the discretion of the Publisher)
which would like to use it for fund-raising purposes.
Contact the publisher for details.
          Publr@KendallNeff.com

Check our website www.WhyDogsAre.com for
feature articles, blogs, stories, reviews and activities.
Share your favorite "dog" charities to be considered
for proceeds donations, and check out our Dog
Stuff!

Dogs weren't always called dogs.
At first, they weren't called anything.

In the beginning, dogs only lived in Heaven. With God.

In Heaven, dogs run forever, chase make-believe cars all day long, and hide bones in big fluffy clouds. Dogs smile a lot in Heaven, too.

A little boy named Brian lived on Earth. He loved to swing on swings. He loved to ride the merry-go-round. He loved to eat pizza just like other kids.

But Brian was born with eyes that did not see and ears that did not hear.

Brian had a wonderful family who loved him very much. God was sure Brian knew how much his family loved him because they took such good care of him. Brian knew his family by their touch.

His sisters lightly touched his shoulders when they were nearby.

His father held his hand.

His mother touched his chest, close to his heart.

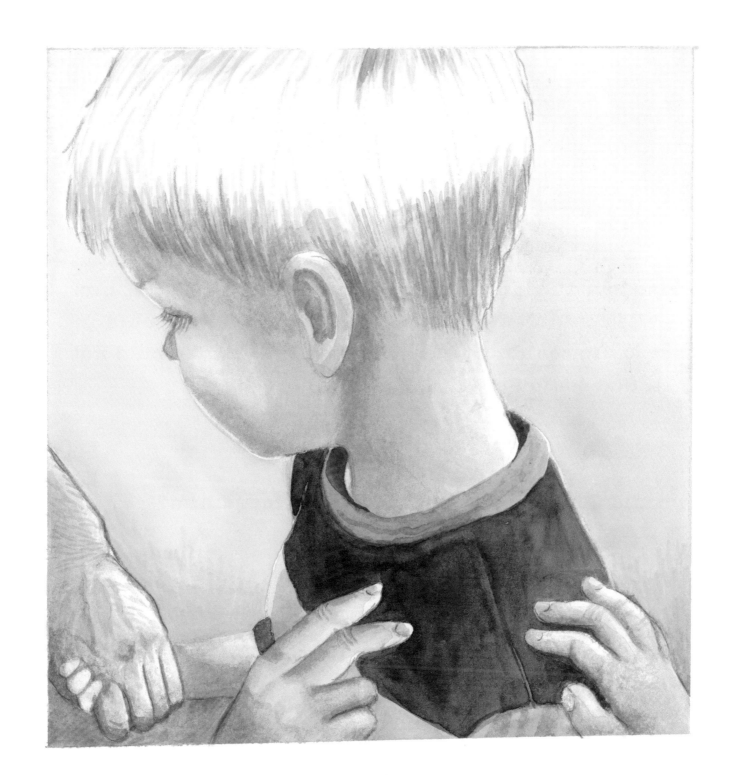

God also loved Brian very much, but how could He let him know? He couldn't send a rainbow because Brian could not see it. He couldn't send a bird to sing—Brian could not hear it. God could not touch Brian.

How could God tell Brian how much He loved him?

One day God called a meeting in Heaven. The angels came, singing joyfully. The rainbows came, dressed in their beautiful colors. The blue skies came, calm and peaceful. The birds came, singing more sweetly than ever.

The dogs took a shortcut and had to jump over some very big clouds, but they arrived just in time and skidded into place.

God explained that He needed help. He needed Brian to know how much He loved him. The angels shouted, "We will go!" So did the rainbows, and the fluffy clouds, and the blue skies. The birds chirped loudly that they could help, too. But God sadly told them that Brian could not see them or hear them.

Then God looked at one of the dogs. He was golden in color. He had big brown eyes and a goofy smile on his face. God called him over to His side, patted him on the head, and said, "I have a very important job for you. You must help Brian know who I am since he cannot see Me or hear Me in the things all around him."

The dog said, "I am not special. I don't even have a name. How can I possibly help Brian?"

God said, "You are the perfect one to do it. Go to Brian and just love him. Stay by his side. Let him lean on you. Help him walk with confidence. Let him hug your neck.

"Teach him these two things: First, to love without expecting anything in return. Second, to forgive those who hurt him—then to forget the hurt and love them even more.

"From now on I will call you DOG—that's GOD spelled backwards!"

DOG began his trip by wagging his tail. He ran through clouds and jumped over a rainbow on his way to Brian's house. God shouted after him, *"If you do a good job, I will send more dogs to Earth!"*

DOG did a _very_ good job.

And that's why... Dogs are.

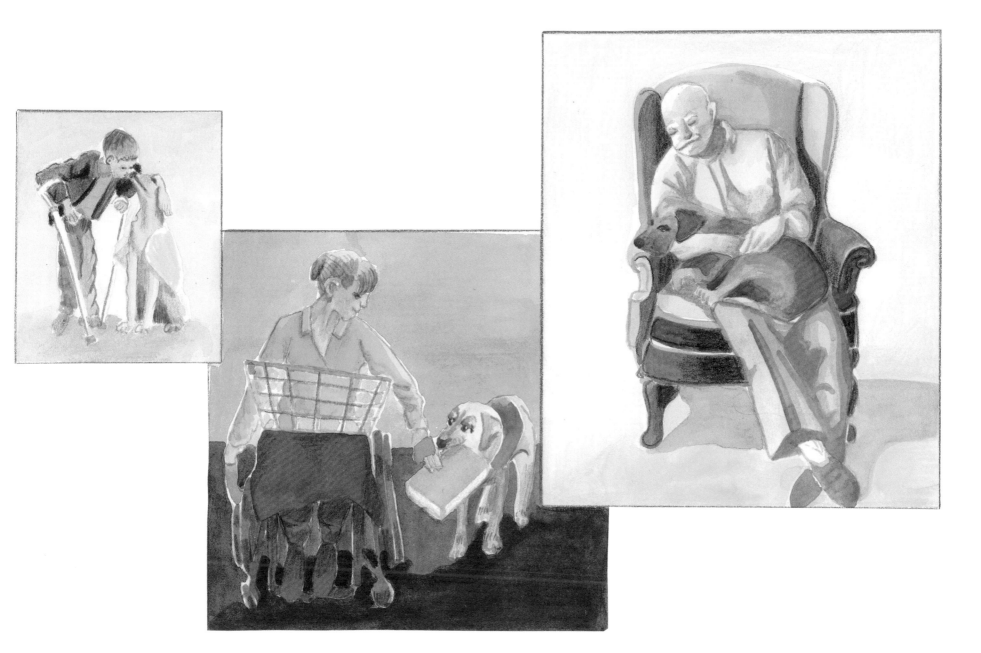